E
SCHMELTZ

DATE DUE

APR 28 94		OCT 2 3 1996
	DEC 04 96	
JUN 25 94		DEC 23 1998
SEP 27 94		
DEC 31 94	JAN 28 97	MAR 29 1999
MAR 22 95	MAR 1 1 97	APR 20 1999
JUN 23 95		JUN 14 1999
JUL 14 95	APR 3 0 97	JUL 0 6 1999
SEP 06 95	JUN 0 5	JUL 16 1999
OCT 0 2 95	JUL 0	AUG 3 0 1999
OCT 21 95	AUG 2 2 1997	SEP 0 9 1999
FEB 06 96	SEP 0 9 1997	MAR 2 1 2000
APR 06 96	NOV 0 4 1997	
MAY 20 96	MAY 0 5 98	
JUN 24 96	JUN 0 2 98	
JUL 18 96	JUL 2 8 1998	
AUG 1 3 96		
AUG 29 96		

OH, SO SILLY!
To librarians, parents, and teachers:

Oh, So Silly! is a Parents Magazine READ ALOUD Original — one title in a series of colorfully illustrated and fun-to-read stories that young readers will be sure to come back to time and time again.

Now, in this special school and library edition of *Oh, So Silly!,* adults have an even greater opportunity to increase children's responsiveness to reading and learning — and to have fun every step of the way.

When you finish this story, check the special section at the back of the book. There you will find games, projects, things to talk about, and other educational activities designed to make reading enjoyable by giving children and adults a chance to play together, work together, and talk over the story they have just read.

For a free color catalog describing Gareth Stevens' list of high-quality books, call 1-800-341-3569 (USA) or 1-800-461-9120 (Canada).

Parents Magazine READ ALOUD Originals:

Golly Gump Swallowed a Fly	Henry's Important Date
The Housekeeper's Dog	Elephant Goes to School
Who Put the Pepper in the Pot?	Rabbit's New Rug
Those Terrible Toy-Breakers	Sand Cake
The Ghost in Dobbs Diner	Socks for Supper
The Biggest Shadow in the Zoo	The Clown-Arounds Go on Vacation
The Old Man and the Afternoon Cat	The Little Witch Sisters
Septimus Bean and His Amazing Machine	The Very Bumpy Bus Ride
Sherlock Chick's First Case	Henry Babysits
A Garden for Miss Mouse	There's No Place Like Home
Witches Four	Up Goes Mr. Downs
Bread and Honey	Bicycle Bear
Pigs in the House	Sweet Dreams, Clown-Arounds!
Milk and Cookies	The Man Who Cooked for Himself
But No Elephants	Where's Rufus?
No Carrots for Harry!	The Giggle Book
Snow Lion	Pickle Things
Henry's Awful Mistake	Oh, So Silly!
The Fox with Cold Feet	The Peace-and-Quiet Diner
Get Well, Clown-Arounds!	Ten Furry Monsters
Pets I Wouldn't Pick	One Little Monkey
Sherlock Chick and the Giant	The Silly Tail Book
Egg Mystery	Aren't You Forgetting Something, Fiona?
Cats! Cats! Cats!	

Library of Congress Cataloging-in-Publication Data

Schmeltz, Susan Alton.
    Oh, so silly! / by Susan Alton Schmeltz ; pictures by Maryann Cocca-Leffler.
      p. cm. -- (Parents magazine read aloud original)
    Summary: A child's variety of experiences on a trip with Grandpa include a plane, a train, the beach, camping, a country fair--and lots of silly things, which the reader may look for in the illustrations.
    ISBN 0-8368-0974-2
    [1. Vacations--Fiction. 2. Stories in rhyme.] I. Cocca-Leffler, Maryann, 1958- ill. II. Title. III. Series.
PZ8.3.S364Oh 1993
[E]--dc20
                                              93-1166

This North American library edition published in 1994 by Gareth Stevens Publishing, 1555 North RiverCenter Drive, Suite 201, Milwaukee, Wisconsin 53212, USA, under an arrangement with Parents Magazine Press, New York.

Text © 1983 by Susan Alton Schmeltz. Illustrations © 1983 by Maryann Cocca-Leffler. Portions of end matter adapted from material first published in the newsletter *From Parents to Parents* by the Parents Magazine Read Aloud Book Club, © 1989 by Gruner + Jahr, USA, Publishing; other portions © 1994 by Gareth Stevens, Inc.

Printed in the United States of America

1 2 3 4 5 6 7 8 9 99 98 97 96 95 94

Oh, So Silly!

A Parents Magazine
Read Aloud Original

Oh, So Silly!

By Susan Alton Schmeltz
pictures by Maryann Cocca-Leffler

Gareth Stevens Publishing • Milwaukee
Parents Magazine Press • New York

Thanks again, P. and T.—S.A.S.

To my husband, Eric—M.C.

Guess what! I'm going on a trip!
My Grandpa's taking me.
So come along and laugh with us
At silly things we'll see.

Our first stop is the airport. I
Just know I'll like to fly.
Oh, look! There's something silly now.
I see it walking by.

The plane is here and it's quite clear
It's not like most I've seen.
Don't point or stare. But look down there.
Do you see what I mean?

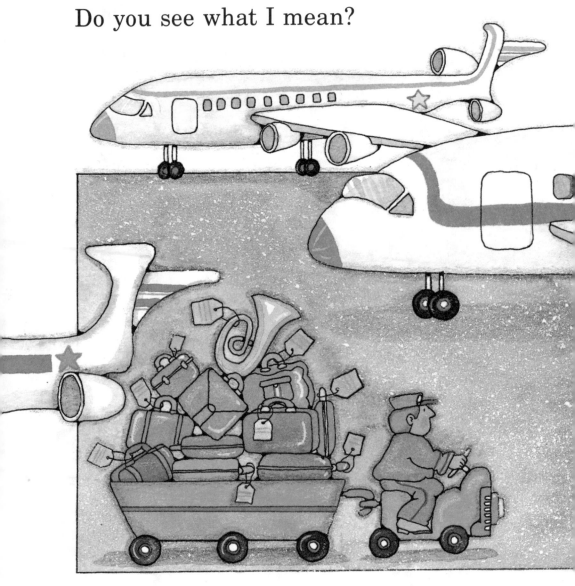

I'm glad we get to climb on board.
We're really on our way!
And soon we'll reach the beach where I
Can run and romp and play.

I love the sea. I love the sand.
I love the salty air.
And just like Grandpa promised, things
Are silly everywhere!

The beach got hot and so we thought
That we would take a swim.
Quick! Tell me! Are things silly here?
Or is the light just dim?

It's time for bed. Lights out. Good night!
Today was really great.
I see a few more silly things.
It must be getting late!

The sun is up and so are we.
We've found a fishing stream.
I think it's even stranger here
Than other spots we've seen!

Tonight we'll eat and sleep outside
Beside this quiet lake.
I wonder. Am I dreaming this?
Or am I wide awake?

Yum! Breakfast in a restaurant.
I hope they'll let us stay
Though we've still got the giggles over
Things from yesterday.

We have a busy time ahead.
Our first stop is the fair.
Are you surprised that silly things
Are happening here and there?

Now Grandpa wants to buy a gift
For me to take back home.
Do you see lots of silly things?
If so, you're not alone!

We're having fun here in the sun,
So won't you join us please?
We've borrowed bikes to ride beside
This grove of silly trees.

A barnyard is the perfect spot
To eat our picnic lunch.
I'll count some sillies while I chew
And chomp and munch and crunch.

It's our last stop. We're heading home,
And though we liked the plane,
My Grandpa thinks it might be fun
To ride back on the train.

This station is a busy place.
They say our train is late.
But I don't mind. Now we can find
More sillies while we wait.

I'll just sit back. The seats are soft.
I know I'll like the view.
Already I am sure I see
A silly thing or two.

We're back at last. Our trip was fun.
I want to go next year!
But now it's nice to be at home...

There's nothing silly here!

Notes to Grown-ups

Major Themes

Here is a quick guide to the significant themes and concepts at work in *Oh, So Silly!*:

- The unexpected can be funny: unexpected events and sights can make us laugh.
- Traveling is fun and exciting: trips are full of new and interesting sights and experiences.
- Order vs. disorder: a child's environment is usually an orderly place where things out of the ordinary can be silly.
- Counting and rhyming: both are orderly activities, and both help children learn conceptual thinking.

Step-by-step Ideas for Reading and Talking

Here are some ideas for further give-and-take between grown-ups and children. The following topics encourage creative discussion of *Oh, So Silly!* and invite the kind of open-ended response that is consistent with many contemporary approaches to reading, including Whole Language:

- A turtle displays the number of silly things included in each picture, and the scenes of silliness progress numerically through the book. See if your child realizes this by asking what the turtle is doing in each scene and throughout the book. Count each scene's silly things with a young child and let an older child count alone.
- Some things pictured in the book are *really* silly, but others are less so. Relationships can be found among some of the objects pictured: the pencil tree, for example. Doesn't the wood from pencils really come from trees? Other examples of less silly things are the pie in the apple tree and the bird cage in yet another tree.

Games for Learning

Games and activities can stimulate young readers and listeners alike to find out more about words, numbers, and ideas. Here are more ideas for turning learning into fun:

Getting a Closer Look

Learning to notice detail is an important part of getting ready to read, and it is a skill children need to help them navigate their environment successfully. Finding all the silly things in the pictures of this book is one way to practice looking at things carefully. Another is to make a photographic map of a small part of your child's world. If you use a simple camera, your child can even snap the pictures himself or herself if you give a little guidance on proper distance and framing.

Take a walk down your block, or through a favorite park or playground. Snap a photo of each house, bend in the path, or piece of playground equipment. Take at least one photo with you in the foreground, another with your child. When the film is developed and the pictures printed, arrange them in the order in which you walked past the different places. You may want to write the addresses, neighbors' names, or labels of gym equipment beneath each picture. Encourage your child to look for things in the pictures not noticed on the walk.

About the Author

SUSAN ALTON SCHMELTZ loves to travel, and she has seen some very silly things. Once, while driving through the state of Washington, she saw a convertible coming toward her. The riders in front looked normal enough, but the full-grown horse in the back seat definitely looked out of place!

About the Artist

MARYANN COCCA-LEFFLER enjoyed illustrating this book because she doesn't get to travel as much as she would like. She and her husband own a greeting card company that features her work.